A NOTE TO PARENTS

When your children are ready to "step into reading," giving them the right books—and lots of them—is as crucial as giving them the right food to eat. **Step into Reading Books** present exciting stories or information reinforced with lively, colorful illustrations that make learning to read fun, satisfying, and worthwhile. They are priced so that acquiring an entire library of them is affordable. And they are beginning readers with an important difference—they're written on three levels.

Step 1 Books, with their very large type and extremely simple vocabulary, have been created for the very youngest readers. **Step 2 Books** are both longer and slightly more difficult. **Step 3 Books,** written to mid-second-grade reading levels, are for the child who has acquired even greater reading skills.

Children develop at different ages. **Step into Reading Books,** with their three levels of reading, are designed to help children become good—and interested—readers *faster*. The grade levels assigned to the three steps—preschool through grade 1 for Step 1, grades 1 through 3 for Step 2, and grades 2 and 3 for Step 3—are intended only as guides. Some children move through all three steps very rapidly; others climb the steps over a period of several years. These books will help your child "step into reading" in style!

Library of Congress Cataloging in Publication Data:
Rosenbloom, Joseph. Deputy Dan and the bank robbers. (Step into reading. A Step 3
book) SUMMARY: Deputy Dan devises a plan to capture a notorious gang of bank robbers.
1. Children's stories, American. [1. Robbers and outlaws—Fiction. 2. West (U.S.)—Fiction.
3. Humorous stories] I. Raglin, Tim, ill. II. Title. III. Series. PZ7.R7197De 1985 [E] 84-15969
ISBN: 0-394-87045-X (trade); 0-394-97045-4 (lib. bdg.)

Manufactured in the United States of America   3 4 5 6 7 8 9 0

STEP INTO READING is a trademark of Random House, Inc.

Step into Reading™

Deputy Dan
and the
BANK ROBBERS

by Joseph Rosenbloom
illustrated by Tim Raglin

A Step 3 Book

Random House 🏠 New York

I live in Gulch City.

Gulch City is a peaceful place.
My job is to keep it that way.

I am the new deputy sheriff.

My name is Dan.

It is Monday, June first. It is hot.

I am sitting in Sheriff Digbee's
office. The sheriff is my boss. We
are having milk and cookies.

We hear a knock.

"Who is that?" Sheriff Digbee asks me.

I say I do not know.

We hear another knock.

"Answer the door," says Sheriff Digbee. "It could be important."

I always follow orders.

I go to the door. I say, "Hello, door!"
"No, NO!" says Sheriff Digbee.
"I did not mean to talk to the door.
I meant to open the door."
"Sure thing, boss!"

I open the door. Elmer Stubbs rushes in. He owns the bank.

"I smell trouble," says Sheriff Digbee.

I sniff. "I do not smell anything," I say.

"No, NO!" says Sheriff Digbee. "I did not mean I smelled something. I meant I could feel trouble was coming."

Elmer Stubbs is out of breath. He waves his arms. "The bank has been robbed!" he shouts.

"I knew it!" says Sheriff Digbee. "BIG trouble!"

Elmer Stubbs sobs. "The robbers took all our money! The bank safe is empty!"

9

"Which way did the robbers go?" asks Sheriff Digbee.

Elmer Stubbs points to the hill outside of town. "They went that way!"

"I will ride to the hill," says Sheriff Digbee. "Deputy Dan, you hop over to the bank. Check the bank for clues."

"You want me to hop over to the bank? You want me to check the bank for clues? Anything you say, boss!"

I start out for the bank. I hop all the way. It is hard work—unless you are a kangaroo or a bunny rabbit.

Elmer Stubbs is back at the bank. He is looking at the empty safe. There are tears in his eyes. I question him.

"Did you see the bank robbers?" I ask.

"Yes," he tells me. "There were four of them. I could not see their faces. They wore masks."

I write in my notebook, "Four masked men."

"Anything more?" I ask.

"Yes," he says. "They were filthy. They needed baths."

I write in my notebook, "Dirty crooks."

Elmer Stubbs shows me a note.
"One of them handed me this," he says.

I read the note.
What does ⬭ mean?
I do not know.
Elmer Stubbs does not know
either.
"Do you want to check the bank
for clues?" he asks.
"I was just going to," I say.

I take a crayon from my pocket.
I check the floor.

I check the walls.

I check the ceiling.

I check the furniture.

I even check Elmer Stubbs. He says it tickles.

I do not find a single clue.

It is Tuesday, June second. It is cloudy.

I am sitting in my boss's office. Elmer Stubbs comes in.

"Did you catch the bank robbers?" he asks Sheriff Digbee.

"No," answers Sheriff Digbee. "I rode to the hills after the robbers. But they got away."

"The stagecoach just brought new money for the bank," Elmer Stubbs tells us. "I am worried about the bank robbers. What if they come back? I will pay you a reward of one thousand dollars if you capture them."

"There must be a way to capture those bank robbers," I think.

"I have a plan," I say. "We can put a sign in the bank window."

I draw a sign.

NEW SHIPMENT OF
MONEY JUST ARRIVED
COME AND GET IT!

"The robbers will see the sign,"
I explain. "They will try to rob
the bank again. This time we will be
ready for them."

"I like your plan," says Sheriff
Digbee.

We put the sign in the bank
window.

BANK

NEW SHIPMENT OF
MONEY JUST ARRIVED
COME AND GET IT!

Sheriff Digbee tells me, "Guard the bank doors, Deputy Dan. Keep them covered at all times."

"You want me to keep the bank doors covered at all times? Okay, boss!"

I go to my house. I gather up my bed sheets. I put them over the bank doors.

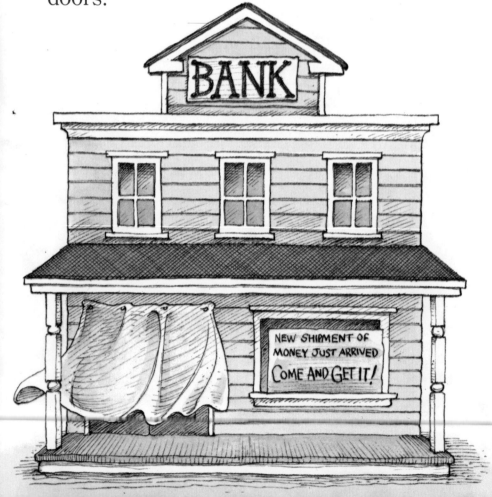

Sheriff Digbee sees the sheets.

"What are you doing, Deputy Dan?" he asks.

"You told me to cover the bank doors, boss. I think the sheets work just fine, don't you?"

"No, NO!" says Sheriff Digbee. "I did not mean to cover the doors with anything. I meant to WATCH the doors."

"Yes, sir!" I say. "I will not take my eyes off those doors!"

3

It is Wednesday, June third. It is windy.

I am standing guard outside the bank.

It is 2:08 P.M.

I see four masked men enter the bank.

It is 2:15 P.M.

I do not see the men leave.

Suddenly Elmer Stubbs comes
running out of the bank.

"The bank has been robbed!"
he shouts.

"Impossible!" I say.

He shows me the safe.

It is empty.

"I do not understand," I tell him.
"I watched the doors all the time.
I did not see anyone come out."

Sheriff Digbee arrives.

"What happened?" he asks.

"The bank has been robbed again!" groans Elmer Stubbs.

"Deputy Dan, did you watch the bank doors?" Sheriff Digbee asks me.

"Of course!" I say.

"Then how did the robbers get away?"

"I don't know, boss."

Elmer Stubbs speaks up. "Maybe the robbers went through the windows."

"Didn't you watch the windows?" Sheriff Digbee asks me.

"No, boss. You told me to watch the doors. So that's what I did."

Sheriff Digbee throws his hat on the ground. He jumps on his hat again and again. Finally he stops.

"Deputy Dan," he says. "There is no time to lose. Pick up your horse. Then come back here."

"You want me to pick up my horse? No problem, boss!"

Did I say no problem? I was wrong.

I try to pick up my horse. I try and I try. I cannot do it. My horse just weighs too much.

I get an idea.

I borrow a crane.

Now it is easy to pick up my
horse.

Sheriff Digbee sees my horse
hanging from the crane.

"For goodness' sake!" he says.
"Why is your horse hanging from
the crane?"

"You told me to pick up my horse. But he was too heavy. So I used a crane."

"No, NO, NO!" shouts Sheriff Digbee. "When I told you to pick up your horse, I meant you should get your horse. I did not mean you should lift your horse up in the air!"

I lower my horse to the ground.

"Now ride to the hill," says
Sheriff Digbee. "And step on it!"

"You want me to ride to the hill?
You want me to step on it? Right
away, boss!"

I ride to the hill.

I get off my horse.

I step on that hill.

I step so hard, I raise clouds of dust.

I hear men grumbling.

"Stop that stepping at once! The dust is getting into our lunch."

I stop.

The dust settles.

I see four men. They are having lunch. They are eating scrambled eggs.

The men are dirty. They need baths.

My mind clicks.

I say, "I know who you are! You are the men who robbed the bank."

"Say, are you looking for trouble?"
they ask.

"Trouble is my business," I answer.

These men are big. These men
are mean. There are four of them.
There is only one of me. But I am not afraid.

I flash my badge.

"I am the new deputy sheriff
of Gulch City," I tell them.

"Disappear!" they growl.
"I will try," I say.
I close my eyes.
"Shazzam!" I say.
I do not disappear.
"Hocus-pocus!" I say.
I do not disappear.
"Poof!" I say.
I still do not disappear.
"Sorry," I say. "I guess I cannot make myself disappear. I will have to arrest you after all."

"You are arresting the wrong men!"
"No, I am not. You are the Scrambled Eggs Gang."
The men turn pale.
"How did you know?"
"That is my secret."

I stare at the men. I stare at them
long and hard. Soon they begin
to shake with fright.

Finally they say, "Okay, you win!"
Then they tell me everything.

They even show me where they hid the stolen money.

The Scrambled Eggs Gang goes to jail.

It is Thursday, June fourth. It is hot.
I am in the sheriff's office.
Elmer Stubbs walks in.
He shakes my hand.
"Thank you," he says. "You
captured those dirty crooks."
"They are not dirty crooks
anymore," I tell him.
"How come?"

"I made them all take baths."

Elmer Stubbs asks, "Deputy Dan, how did you know those men were the bank robbers?"

"Easy," I say. "The men who robbed the bank were dirty. So were the men I captured."

Elmer Stubbs shakes his head. "Just because a person is dirty doesn't make him a bank robber."

"True," I reply. "But there is more."

I show Elmer Stubbs a piece of paper.

"Remember this?" I ask.

Elmer Stubbs says, "It is the note the robbers handed me. But I still do not know what  means."

"Look again," I tell him.

He studies the note.

"These letters are scrambled," says Elmer Stubbs. "They spell EGGS."

"So?"

"Now I understand!" Elmer
Stubbs cries. "SCRAMBLED EGGS!
This must be the sign of the
Scrambled Eggs Gang!"

Elmer Stubbs writes a check.

"Here is the thousand-dollar
reward, Deputy Dan. Take it. It is yours."

"Sorry," I tell him. "I cannot take money for doing my job."

Elmer Stubbs says, "We can use the reward money any way you like."

I think for a moment. "It would be nice to use the money to bring a free circus to Gulch City."

"A free circus is a wonderful idea!" says Sheriff Digbee.

Elmer Stubbs smiles. "I love the circus. I might even run away with it when it gets here."

"Better not!" I warn.

"Why not?" he asks.

"Because I would make you bring it right back!"

Everyone laughs.

Gulch City is peaceful again.

And that's the way I, Deputy Dan, like it.